Level: 4.9
PT: 2.0
Quiz: 149349

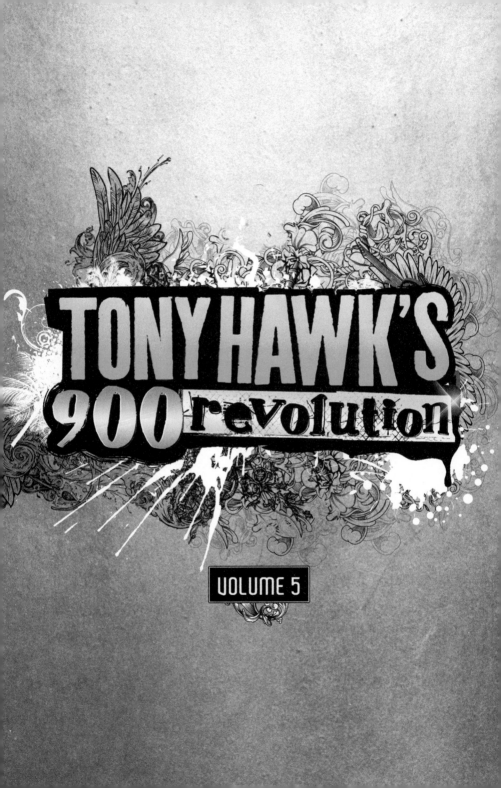

Tony Hawk's 900 Revolution
is published by Stone Arch Books
a Capstone imprint, 1710 Roe Crest Drive, North Mankato,
MN 56003 www.capstonepub.com Copyright © 2012
by Stone Arch Books All rights reserved. No part of this
publication may be reproduced in whole or in part, or stored
in a retrieval system, or transmitted in any form or by any
means, electronic, mechanical, photocopying, recording, or
otherwise, without written permission of the publisher.

Cataloging-in-Publication Data is available on the Library
of Congress website.
ISBN: 978-1-4342-3311-0 (library binding)
ISBN: 978-1-4342-3887-0 (paperback)

Summary: As a new chapter begins, the first four members
of the Revolution team — Omar, Dylan, Amy, and Joey
— search for next piece of Tony Hawk's powerful 900
skateboard. Their journey takes them to the American
Midwest, where a rock-n-roll teen tunes in to the
mysterious Artifact's location. Unfortunately, when another
gang of teens, known as the Collective, follows them on
their quest, the dangers are suddenly amplified.

Photo and Vector Graphics Credits: Shutterstock.
Photo credit page 122, Bart Jones/ Tony Hawk,
Photo credit page 123, Karon Dubke/ Capstone..

Art Director: Heather Kindseth
Cover and Interior Graphic Designer: Kay Fraser
Comic Insert Graphic Designer: Hilary Walcholz

Printed in the United States of America in Stevens Point,
Wisconsin.
102011
006404WZS12

TONY HAWK'S 900 revolution

AMPLIFIED

BY BLAKE A. HOENA // ILLUSTRATED BY WILSON TORTOSA

VOLUME 5

STONE ARCH BOOKS
a capstone imprint

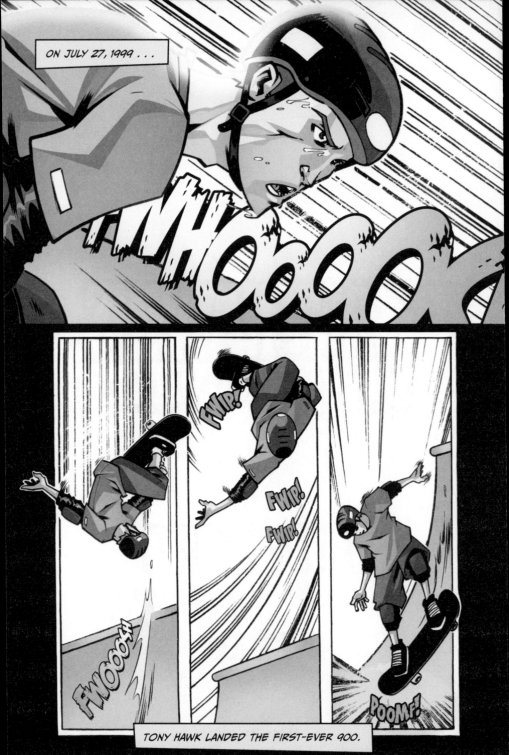

1

"Okay, so what're we doing up here in the Great White North?" Dylan asked.

"Just scoping out the local talent," Amy replied.

The pair of teens leaned against the outer fence of Brackett Skatepark in Minneapolis. Dylan, wearing khakis, a Birdhouse tee, and a Yankees ball cap, toed his board back and forth. Amy, in jeans and a black hoodie, held hers upright by its nose. The park was filled on the sunny Saturday afternoon, and the teens took in the layout of the street course. There were a couple of flat bars, stairs, some ramps, and a quarter pipe — nothing too outrageous.

A skater approached the railing nearest them as if he were about to execute a grind.

The kid's toe caught the railing as he ollied up, and he belly-flopped on to the pavement. Dylan and Amy both cringed as the kid stood, wiping bloody palms on his pants.

"Again, what're we doing here, really?" Dylan asked.

"I told you, Omar asked us to check out the local skaters," Amy replied. "He and Joey are researching the location of the next Fragment."

Dylan and Amy, along with their friends Omar and Joey, were part of a secret organization called the Revolution. Omar was kind of their leader, or at least the member of the group who knew the most about the Revolution's mission — to find the pieces of the board that Tony Hawk used to perform the first-ever 900.

Amy wasn't sure she understood what had happened next, but as Tony held the skateboard up in celebration of completing that awesome trick, the skateboard had exploded. Pieces of it were now scattered throughout the world. Their goal was to gather the Fragments because each one held a secret power. A power that would be dangerous in the wrong hands.

Amy was still a little surprised to be part of something so big. Dylan seemed to take it for granted.

"Aw, come on," Dylan continued. "These skaters are just a bunch of newbs."

Dylan's right, Amy thought as they watched the skaters perform simple kickflips and grinds. Kids wobbled and fell and crashed. It was a circus. The group was probably wasting their time here.

"Hey, look," Dylan said as he pointed at a kid awkwardly balancing on his board and grinning. "He just did a *gollie!*"

"A what?" Amy asked.

"A gollie," Dylan explained. "As in, 'Golly gee, I just did an ollie without falling on my butt!'"

"Give them a break, Dylan," Amy said.

"That's Slider," Dylan corrected.

"Oh, I forgot to call you by your silly nickname," Amy said. "Lay off, *Slider.* These kids didn't grow up with the streets of New York as their skatepark. They also don't have a certain something that you do."

Amy's eyes drifted from Dylan's face to his board. If anyone bothered to look closely, they'd notice that the tail didn't quite match the rest of the deck. That was Dylan's Fragment — the tail of Tony's 900 board — attached to his own. Amy's hand slid into her front pocket, where she kept hers. She rubbed her fingers against a familiar piece of deck, felt the splintered wood against her fingers, and received a jolt of power that felt like electricity. It was intoxicating.

"Well, while we're here, I'm gonna make the best of it," Dylan said. He kicked his board forward and leaped onto it. He slowly coasted toward a flat bar.

Dylan frustrated Amy. He was just an arrogant show-off. Even worse, he was cute enough to make her forget that he was an arrogant show-off. With one flash of his smile, Amy felt a queasiness start to build in her stomach. The good kind of queasy. The kind you felt on a roller coaster just as your car was tipping over the first drop. Problem is, every time Amy caught herself smiling at something Dylan said or did, she suddenly remembered a certain someone whom she'd had to leave behind in order to join the Revolution. Her feelings quickly turned sour.

"Just don't draw attention to yourself. . . ." Amy's voiced trailed off as she yelled after Dylan.

Too late.

As Dylan neared the flat bar, he kicked his board up and did 5-0 grind across its length. Amy knew that was a deliberate trick. Difficult, yet done with such ease that it told the other skaters to make room. They were going to be schooled.

Dylan headed straight for the closest ramp. At its top, he spun a backside 360 ollie and then headed toward the nearest rail.

Dylan then popped his skateboard up. He did a frontside feeble across the entire rail, landing the trick perfectly.

He may have been an arrogant show-off, but Dylan Crow was good. Amy had to admit that. She just hoped nobody noticed the trace of blue electricity that followed Dylan's skateboard from trick to trick.

Dylan ran through a few other tricks. Some Amy couldn't even name. As skaters gathered to watch, he did a nose stall at the top of a ramp to check out the crowd. This was his moment. Dylan had their attention. Now, he was going do something big.

Amy felt a brush on her shoulder, almost like the flutter of wings.

"Is that your friend?" a voice whispered in her ear.

Amy turned to see a pixyish girl with spiky hair and tube-sock arm bands.

"Um, yeah," Amy replied, distracted.

Just then, the crowd of skaters hooted and hollered. Amy turned, but Dylan had already landed his trick. "Dang, I missed it," she muttered to herself.

"So what do you want?" she turned back toward the girl, sounding more annoyed then she meant to.

"I-I-," the girl stammered. "He's pretty good. Does he ride for anyone?"

Amy should have known it. Another groupie falling for the good-looking, arrogant show-off.

"Yeah, he's with a team. We both are," Amy replied.

"Really, you, too?" asked the girl.

"Yeah, but I'm more into powder than pavement."

Just then, Dylan skated up to them, all sweaty and out of breath.

"Who's your friend?" he asked Amy as he flashed the pixyish girl a smile.

"I'm Wren," she replied, more to Amy than Dylan.

"Listen, we should get going, don't you think, Ames?" Dylan asked. "People to see. Rails to grind. You know — that sort of thing."

"Oh, I'm sorry if I'm keeping you," Wren said, looking down at her feet and sounding nervous. "Here." Wren pulled a crumbled flyer out of her pocket and handed it to Amy. It read:

Amateur Night @ First Ave

18 and under show

"If you're checking out the local skater scene, a lot of folks will be there," Wren said. "I'll be there."

"Maybe we'll stop by," Amy replied, casually.

Amy and Dylan turned away from Wren and then hopped on their boards, speeding away from the park.

"So what was that all about?" Dylan asked Amy.

"Not sure. Just a groupie, I guess," she replied.

"Did you ask if she skated? I thought Omar said we were looking for a skater girl," Dylan added.

"No, but she invited us to this," Amy handed the flyer to Dylan. "She'll be there."

"Looks like we might have some fun here after all," said Dylan with a smile.

2

Meanwhile, in Minneapolis's sister city, Saint Paul, Joey Rail was thrumming his fingers against a table, impatiently. "Seriously, why did we get research duty, Omar?" he asked. "Slider and Amy get to hit the skateparks."

"There's just something I need to find out," Omar replied. "Plus, I'd hate to imagine what trouble you and Dylan would get into if you were left on your own."

The pair sat outside a coffee shop, each with a computer tablet on his lap.

"Hey, you're cool being plugged in and sipping your green tea," Joey said. "But I'd rather be hitting some trails, sweating, and covered in mud."

"It's got antioxidants." Omar held up his cup of tea.

"Seriously, you West Coasters and your health food," Joey said, rolling his eyes.

Omar leaned close to whisper in Joey's ear, as if he were afraid someone might overhear him.

"You don't get it, Joey," Omar explained. "Ever since I touched that first Fragment, I've been having these visions. They're kind of like movie previews with no sound tracks. This time, I saw the Mississippi River, a girl skater, and caves. I'm not sure how they all tie in, but they're clues to the location of the next Fragment."

"You're like a human GPS," Joey said with a laugh. "So what have you found?"

"This," Omar said, and then showed Joey his tablet.

The header on the top of Omar's screen read: "Wabasha Street Caves." Joey leaned over to touch a link. A map popped up with the location of the caves.

"That's only a few miles from here," Joey said, tracing his finger along the map.

"Shall we?" Omar said with a wink.

"Yeah, let's get going," Joey replied.

The teens each tucked their tablets into packs, and then slung them over their shoulders. Omar pulled his board out from under his chair. Joey walked over to where his BMX bike leaned against the coffee shop.

After Joey got on his bike, he turned to Omar. "Ready to do some tailgating, BMX style?" he asked.

Omar stepped on his board and coasted over to Joey. He grabbed the back of Joey's seat, and they were off.

Joey peddled fast, hopped curbs, and wove his way through traffic, almost as if he had forgotten Omar was tagging along. So Omar had to pay close attention and yell "sorry" more than a couple of times as he had several near misses with people. But it seemed that every time they approached a curb or a bench, Joey would pause just enough for Omar to do an ollie or other trick and then grab back on.

Omar started to look for the next trick — a rail to grind or a curb to hop. He was having fun, sweating under the summer sun and letting the wind whip his hair back as they raced through downtown Saint Paul.

Suddenly, Joey darted to the right, too quick for Omar. He lost his grip on the bike seat. Straight ahead was a black-and-white fluff ball. Without thinking, Omar kicked up his board, jumping over the pooch, and completed a frontside180. The dog's owner started screaming at him.

Omar didn't even look back. Sadly, he was used to this type of treatment from his days of skateboarding on the piers of San Diego.

Non-skateboarders everywhere seemed to have it out for skateboarders like him, whether they were causing problems or not.

Joey zipped in front of him so Omar could grab his bike seat. He dared a quick glance at Omar. "She just bust a vein?" he asked. Then he dug in, pedaling hard.

Joey turned into the bike lane of a busy street, and the city opened up into a wide river valley. Skyscrapers shrunk behind them as Joey pedaled up a bridge that crossed the Mississippi River. Omar was glad Joey was doing all the work.

Soon, they reached the apex of the bridge, and Joey pumped the pedals, building up steam. Omar crouched low as they sped down the other side of the bridge. He wasn't used to going this fast on his board, but the speed was invigorating.

Once across the bridge, the road got a little rough, so they hopped up on the sidewalk. Omar was concentrating on avoiding the cracks in the concrete when Joey skidded to a halt. Omar shot past him, unable to stop for nearly a quarter of a block. Doing a 180, he pushed his board back toward where Joey waited.

"Jerk." Omar laughed as he reached Joey.

Joey smirked.

"So why we are stopping?" Omar asked.

Joey nodded toward a parking lot filled with cars. Beyond that was a large wooden door with a sign that read: "Wabasha Street Caves."

Suddenly, Omar heard the screech of a hawk nearby, and the world around him disappeared. What he saw took his breath away. He was soaring hundreds of feet above the ground, following the twists of a mighty river. The people below, walking along the banks of the water, were ant-like specs.

The hawk screeched again, sounding as it if were right next to him. Omar turned his head to look around. All he saw against the blue sky was a wing — feathers ruffling in the wind. That wing extended from where his shoulder should be.

Below him, the small dot of a songbird darted through the air. Instinct took hold, and Omar dove. As he plunged toward the bird and reached out his talons, it looked up at him and screamed — not a bird scream, but a human one, loud and piercing.

Then he felt the sky around him split apart. He was no longer flying, but standing in front of a dark pit that went down and down into complete darkness.

3

Joey didn't know what he should be more worried about. Omar in some kind epileptic shock or the van in the corner of the parking lot. The vehicle's windows were tinted and radio antennas covered its roof like a porcupine. It looked suspiciously like something the evil Collective would be snooping around in.

Joey hunched down behind a car, trying to pull Omar along with him. His friend was having another one of his visions and wouldn't budge — oblivious to the danger at hand.

"Omar," he whispered. "Come on, man."

Joey yanked on Omar's arm, but his friend just stared up at the sky with glazed eyes. Joey didn't know what to do.

"Omar!" Joey said a little louder. "It's go time."

Joey heard a car lock beep. He peeked over the hood of the car he was hiding behind, fearing the worst. One of the side doors of the black van slid open, and a member of the Collective poked his head out.

"Find out anything," the man shouted.

Joey scanned the parking lot to see who he was talking to. Three men and one woman, all dressed in black and wearing dark sunglasses, had just exited the door to the Wabasha Street Caves and were crossing the parking lot. Omar was still out in the open, easily seen. All the members of the Collective had to do was look to their right.

"Omar!" Joey screamed through his teeth and tugged on his friend's arm.

Nothing.

Then the sound of four sets of feet skidding to a halt sent shivers down Joey's spine.

Crap! he thought.

"Well, well," one of the Collective agents said. "Looks like this mission is getting easier by the minute. "Get him!"

Two of the Collective members drew Taser sticks from their belts and then sprinted toward Omar. The other two raced to the van.

"Omar!" Joey shouted.

Nothing.

Joey jumped up from his hiding spot. *Whack!* He slapped Omar across the face.

Nothing.

Joey wound up again. Before he could strike, Omar's eyes blinked open. He was back in the real world.

"Grab on," Joey shouted as he leaped onto his bike.

Omar had been through enough sticky situations. He didn't even ask why. He just did it, hopping on his board and then grabbing the back of Joey's seat. Joey dug in, pumping the pedals hard and dragging Omar along with him. A Taser stick crackled overhead as one of the Collective took a swipe at Omar.

The two Collective agents on foot were easy to ditch. The others, running for the van, would be another story. Then there was the driver . . .

The van's engine roared to life as the two Collective agents dove through the side door. The van then lurched forward, hopping the curb. Cars screeched and swerved as the van rambled into the street.

Now things are going to get interesting, Joey thought.

Joey headed back the way they had come. He knew there were side streets up ahead, and recalling the map he had seen earlier, some of those led to a bike path.

Just blocks into the chase, Joey felt the burn in his legs. They had been riding for a few miles already and pulling the additional weight of Omar took quite an effort. His friend must have sensed this. As Joey leaned left, taking a sharp turn onto a side street, Omar shouted, "Split up!"

All of a sudden, the extra drag disappeared, and Joey shot forward. He dared a glance back, to see what had happened to Omar, but his friend must have headed in the opposite direction. There was no sign of him.

Joey didn't have time to worry about Omar, though. Tires squealing, the black van wheeled around the corner, taking the same turn he had just made.

Time to focus, Joey thought to himself. The road sloped down. Joey leaned forward and pushed into the pedals, building up speed. He couldn't worry that the van was gaining on him. He needed to keep his eye out for where the bike trail intersected the road.

Without realizing it, Joey's left hand drifted toward the pendant he wore around his neck. Blue electricity surrounded his fist. This was where he kept his Fragment — a ball bearing from Tony's 900 board.

Energy coursed through Joey like he had just grabbed hold of a power line. He felt a burst of electricity spread throughout his body.

Joey felt the world around him come alive. He could sense that the grill of the van was only meters behind him. He could see the sliver of pavement that was the bike trail up ahead.

He leaned right, turning sharply, and darted toward the path. The whoosh of the van speeding past nearly threw him off balance. But he made it. Now he raced along the bike trail — the road to his left and the Mississippi River to his right — with no idea what lay ahead.

Omar let go of Joey's bike seat and leaned hard right. The bridge that crossed the Mississippi River rose up in front of him. No way he could escape in that direction. He'd be too out in the open.

Earlier, when he and Joey had crossed the bridge, Omar had noticed a small island below. The island had a park and band shell. People were gathering in front of the stage, and he hoped that the crowd had grown large enough for him to hide in.

Omar leaned left when he saw the walkway that led down to the river's bank. He crouched low and let gravity build up his speed. *A long board would be perfect right now,* he thought.

Soon enough, Omar was starting to come across random groups of people, and he had to weave his way through them. They were heading toward the footbridge that crossed over to the island. Omar didn't like the idea of heading anywhere without a clear escape route, but he had no choice. Looking back in the direction he had just come from, he saw two of the Collective agents were casually walking down the hill and toward the island, their leisurely pace a sure sign that they felt they had snared their prey.

The one thing that kept Omar moving forward, though, was a bird circling over the island like a beacon calling him to safety. It was a grebe, a type of waterfowl common out west, and his namesake — Grebes, as in Omar Grebes.

I didn't know they lived this far north, Omar thought.

Omar crossed the bridge and then hopped off his skateboard. The crowd on the island had grown, but now he needed to blend in.

The band on stage was warming up. Omar recognized the rhythmic beat of their drums — ska, music he loved. He also noticed the reds and oranges and yellows of the clothing that surrounded him. He stood out like a sore thumb, wearing his black T-shirt and carrying a skateboard.

He yanked the front wheel from his board. The wheel sizzled with blue energy. This was his Fragment — his piece of Tony's 900 board. He stuffed the wheel into his front pocket before ditching his board under the footbridge.

On the outskirts of the park stood several tents. Vendors sold everything from fried food on a stick to kufis and other paraphernalia. For a moment, the aromas of food caused his stomach to lurch, but he couldn't imagine anything here would be better than the fish tacos he bought on the pier back home. Instead, he headed for one of the T-shirt vendors. There he bought a brightly colored tie-dye. Stripping his shirt, he stuffed it into his pack and donned his new duds.

In front of him, a girl stood watching him exchange shirts. She smiled as Omar caught her looking.

"Hey, what's up?" Omar asked, smiling back.

"Nothing. Just, um —" she giggled as she bit her lower lip. "Enjoying the show."

Omar flushed.

In the background, the rhythms of the band piped up. On the footbridge, the two Collective members were pushing their way past the people on the walkway. Omar knew it was either time to call for backup or try to blend into the crowd.

Omar reached for his pack, felt the small two-way radio there, but chose not to pull it out. He had become a part of something dangerous, and if he was going to ride this out, he couldn't be calling for help every time he got into a sticky situation. He opted for plan B.

"Care to dance?" Omar asked the girl.

"You don't even know my name," she replied.

Grabbing her hand, Omar responded, "let's see if you can dance first. Then, I'll get your name."

Omar was surprised at his confidence. But desperate times took desperate measures. He was even more surprised when the girl tightened her grip on his hand and followed him toward the stage.

*   *   *

Meanwhile, Joey wasn't having as easy of a time as Omar. The Collective van swerved, hopped the curb, and was on the bike path behind him.

While to his right lay a wide-open grassy park, to his left, luckily, a narrow row of trees sprouted up. To avoid the van, Joey decided to take things off trail. He saw a gap between some birches and hit it at full speed. The van couldn't follow through the thicket. Once passed the trees, he was back on the road, and now the van was on the bike path.

Irony? Joey thought.

The line of trees thickened, forcing the van further and further away from the road. As Joey watched it flashing between tree trunks, he saw the van's back door swing open. A ramp slid out and scrapped against the bike path, sending sparks flying in all directions. Two small dirt bikes then darted down the ramp.

"Crap!" Joey cursed again. While the van had the edge on speed, he had the advantage of mobility. He could turn faster and get places the van couldn't. The dirt bikes took that advantage away. They could go anywhere he could . . . only faster.

The dirt bike engines roared as their riders whipped them around, and then they cut through the trees toward Joey. The teen quickly surveyed his surroundings. To his right were trees and the bike path. A park and the Mississippi River was just beyond that — no escape there unless he wanted to swim for it. To his left was a tree-lined ridge, about fifty meters high. Somehow that'd have to be his way out. As he sped down the road, Joey watched for a path that might lead up. What he found was a narrow dirt track that had been eroded away by water. It was his chance.

Joey hit the hill at full speed, felt the knobs on his tires bite dirt, and climbed as fast as he could.

The climb was slow going, but this was the type of riding he was used to — trail riding, where his tires kicked up mud and dirt, and one slip meant a hard fall with bruises or broken bones as a reward.

The riders on the dirt bikes weren't far behind. They rapidly covered the distance between the van and Joey. Then they began their climb.

The first motorcyclist was impatient — he came at the hill too fast. As soon as his back tire hit dirt, it spun, lifting the front tire in the air. The bike flipped, falling back onto the rider.

The other rider was more cautious. She stood on her pegs and leaned forward, keeping the front tire down on the path. She was speeding up the hill after him.

Joey knew he wasn't going to win this race. No matter what sort of power the Fragment gave him, he'd never out-pedal an experienced rider on a dirt bike.

Joey stopped and then reached into his pack, pulling out a two-way radio. He was about ten meters above the girl motorcyclist, and he had just a moment to spare.

"I need an extraction," he shouted into the radio. Flipping on the radio's homing signal, he jammed the two-way into his front pocket.

Instead of climbing, he spun his bike around and headed back down the hill over rough terrain.

Again, he felt the energy of his Fragment come alive. Felt the openings in the trees. Sensed the ruts in the ground. And he picked the perfect downhill path.

Joey shot across the road, through the line of trees, over the bike path, and across the stretch of grass beyond that. Not the black van. Not the girl on the dirt bike. Nobody could catch him now before he reached his goal. All that was between him and the river was a guardrail.

His bike crashed into the gray metal, and then he flew over the handlebars. For a brief moment, he floated in the air. During that instant, he swore he saw a rail — a small brown marsh bird — sitting in the tall grass along the bank of the river. He thought that it must be a sign of luck for him, Joey Rail.

Then darkness crashed down around him.

5

Dylan stood with Amy outside a black building in downtown Minneapolis. He was mindlessly looking up, watching a crow bob its head up and down. The bird cawed loudly at the growing crowd.

You must be the opening act, Dylan thought. *If only I had some popcorn for you.*

The crow sat atop a billboard, which read:

Amateur Night @ First Ave
18 and under show

The line to get inside wound around the block, and Dylan was getting frustrated. He had hoped that being in the Revolution would come with privileges, like getting to move to the front of the line at shows and snagging some VIP seats. No such luck.

Instead, Dylan was standing amongst a lot of skater wannabes. What was even more annoying, they were all dressed similarly to him — khaki shorts, some skater tees, and many with ball caps askew, like his. Those wearing Twins hats seemed to be scowling at his Yankees cap.

"When's the last time they won the World Series?" he growled at one group of kids.

"Dylan, chill," Amy said. "What's up with the attitude?"

Dylan toed the pavement in front of him and adjusted the pack that was slung over his shoulder. In it, he carried his board. He almost felt uncomfortable on two feet instead of four wheels, but there were "no skateboarding" signs all over the area. And big burly guys with crossed arms were standing around to enforce that rule.

"Just impatient," Dylan said. "All this standing around and no action."

"Would you rather be behind a computer, like Omar and Joey, on research duty?" Amy asked.

"No."

"Then chill," Amy said. "We're almost in. And from the looks of this crowd, nearly every skater in town is here tonight."

"Still no word from Omar?" Dylan asked.

"Not a text," Amy replied.

Dylan and Amy had not heard from Joey or Omar since that morning, when they'd discussed their plans for the day. It was now eight at night. Dylan doubted that Joey, or even Omar, could stare at a computer screen that long.

As the line inched forward, the thump of music began to reverberate. Dylan was used to being in a crowded city — having grown up in New York — but he wasn't comfortable being in the thick of a group of people like he was now. Without his board under foot, he felt helpless.

When they entered the building, security guards checked their bags. Luckily, they had ditched everything but their boards, a spare hoodie each, and a two-way radio disguised as a cell phone. They didn't dare bring any gadgets that could give them away as being anything more than a couple of normal skater kids.

Inside, the beat of the music washed over them in waves. The place was lit with red and blue and yellow floodlights, and it was standing room only. Dylan and Amy jostled their way through the crowd and found an area where they could stand and talk briefly.

"Now what?" Dylan screamed in Amy's ear.

"I don't know," Amy yelled back.

Dylan rolled his eyes.

"Without Omar, I'm as lost as you are," Amy said.

"Okay, then, I'm going to wander." With that, Dylan turned from Amy and disappeared into the crowd.

Moments like these made Amy wonder if she really wouldn't better off back home. She felt so out of her league in this new world. Sure, the mountains in Colorado had their dangers, hidden beneath drifts of snow. At least she had grown to understand them, recognize them, and even felt she could tackle them when the need arose. Here, she felt lost. She didn't know what she was doing. She didn't know what sort of dangers lay ahead.

Amy pulled the drawn strings of her hoodie tight, causing its hood to cover her face. She dropped her fists to her sides. As she stood there, frustrated, she felt a warm, soft hand slide into hers. It was smaller than hers, and she didn't know why, but she let its fingers pry her fist open. When their hands were entwined, she turned to see Wren looking up at her and smiling.

"I knew you'd come," Wren said.

"Then do you know what I'm supposed to be doing here?" Amy asked.

"Dancing," Wren replied.

"Huh?"

"Dance with me," Wren said. "Come on."

Wren tugged Amy toward the stage. In front of the band, a crowd of teens had gathered. They danced wildly to the thick rhythms of the music. Arms flailed. Hips grooved. Heads shook. Hair flew. Wren freely gave herself to the music. Amy could think of nothing better to do than join her and let the music drown out the worries and self doubt that whirled about her head.

* * *

Meanwhile, Dylan wove his way through the crowd. He didn't know what he was looking for, or whom. He just hoped that instincts or his Fragment would give him some sort of signal.

He was struggling with this teamwork thing. When he'd joined the Revolution, he didn't know he was going to be paired up with Omar, Joey, and Amy. He had been hoping he'd get to do things on his own, like he had done growing up in the streets of New York City.

Too many times he had trusted someone, and too many times he had been let down. That's just what happens when you grow up as a foster kid. You get tossed around from home to home. It was easier not having to depend on anyone.

As Dylan was lost in his thoughts, he didn't noticed a large figure step in front of him. Dylan ran smack into the guy's back.

"Hey, watch it, jerk!" the guy growled as he turned on Dylan.

Dylan froze. He recognized that voice — Buzzer, one of the Collective agents. Dylan had outsmarted him and a couple of Buzzer's buddies back in NYC to get his Fragment.

Dylan kept his head down, letting his baseball cap's brim hide his face.

"Sorry, man," Dylan muttered, and then quickly stepped into the swarm of people that filled the venue. He was thankful that Buzzer didn't pursue any trouble.

Once he was a few people deep in the crowd, Dylan risked a glance back. Buzzer had resumed talking to a group of two girls and one other guy. They were all dressed in black and wearing dark sunglasses.

What's he doing here? Dylan wondered. And as he did, he was thankful Amy was near at hand. *There's safety in numbers. If only Omar and Joey were here to even up the odds.*

6

With each beat of the music, Omar felt Shawna's body slide close. She had told him her name after the first song. Now, he had completely forgotten how long they'd been dancing.

Out of the corner of his eye, he kept watch on the dark dressed figures that patrolled the outskirts of the island. At first there had only been two of them, but their numbers had grown to five. That accounted for all the Collective agents he and Joey had initially run into, so he was hoping that his teammate had escaped. Now it was his turn.

"If you're not gonna pay attention to me, I'm not gonna dance with you," Shawna said.

"Huh?" Omar replied.

She stood before him, hips cocked and arms crossed.

"That whole last song, you were eyeing those men in black instead of me," she said.

Omar grabbed her arms and pulled her close. "Sorry, I just . . ." He wasn't sure what to tell her. What he could tell her?

She whispered in his ear, "Are you in trouble?"

He nodded.

"Cops?" she asked.

He shook his head. "Worse."

"Well then, there's three ways off this island," she explained. "The footbridge."

She nodded in the direction of the bridge Omar had crossed earlier. A Collective member stood at the foot of it.

"Those steps," she said, nodding in the direction of a support pillar for the bridge that Joey and Dylan had used to cross the Mississippi earlier that day. At its base stood another Collective agent, who waited in front of a staircase that spiraled upward.

"Or swim?" Omar asked.

Shawna scrunched up her face. "In the Mississippi? No way, it stinks like fish. My friends and I have a canoe back behind the booth where you bought that shirt."

"Well, let's go," Omar said.

Avoiding the Collective agents was fairly easy as long as he knew where they were. Keeping up with Shawna wasn't. She headed straight for the T-shirt stand like she hadn't a worry in the world.

But maybe that's it, Omar thought. *Act like you belong to avoid drawing attention to yourself.*

They wove their way through the crowd of people. Shawna then told her friends at the T-shirt booth that she needed to borrow the canoe to get Omar off the island. Her friends shot her some teasing winks, but they didn't make much of a fuss.

Omar felt the canoe wobble as he stepped into it. Carefully, he made his way to the front seat. Shawna pushed off and then jumped into the back. Quietly, they paddled away from the island. Omar hoped that with the sun setting, it was too dark for anyone to notice them leaving.

They were only about two hundred meters downstream of the island when Omar noticed two black specs ahead of them skimming along the surface of the water, headed in their direction. Omar scanned the area around them. He was half hoping to see, soaring overhead, the grebe he had spotted earlier. He was searching for a sign to tell him what to do.

Whoever was headed in their direction was still far off, and Omar and Shawna were probably only a hundred yards from shore.

"Let's head for it," Omar yelled to Shawna. He didn't want to take any chances.

They dug their paddles into the water, and the canoe cut through the waves. Those black specs grew increasingly larger — and fast. By the time he heard the roar of their engines, they were close enough for him to tell that they were personal watercrafts, with three riders. And Omar could tell that they had altered their course and were headed in their direction. He hoped it wasn't more Collective agents.

The river's bank was teasingly close when the watercrafts caught up with them. Omar was still so intent on paddling that he didn't noticed when a familiar face pulled up alongside him.

"Omar, stop."

"Eldrick?" Omar's gaped in surprise. "What are you doing here?"

Back home, Eldrick had introduced Omar to the Revolution. He now served as a mentor to the crew.

Then Omar looked over at the other watercrafts. While he didn't recognize the driver, he was close friends with the passenger.

"Joey!" Omar exclaimed. "Glad to see you got away."

"With a little help," Joey said as he nodded toward Eldrick.

"We've been searching the river bank for you for nearly an hour," Eldrick explained. "We would've found you quicker if you had hit your homing signal."

Omar leaped onto the back of Eldrick's watercrafts. On one hand, he was relieved that Joey was safe. On the other, he was disappointed that Eldrick had to come to the rescue. This was supposed to be his mission. His test. His chance to prove to everyone in the Revolution that he could handle whatever came his way. Yet, here he was, being rescued again.

Before Omar could do anything more than say thanks to Shawna, they were off.

Amy Kestrel was sweating and exhausted. Dancing had worn her out as much as a difficult run down the slopes. Yet, this was a freeing sort of exhaustion. She didn't need to worry about whether her legs would give out on a mogul or if there was an unforeseen chasm under the snow. She could just dance and be herself.

No worries.

During the last song, Amy had lost sight of Wren. When the song had ended, the band exited in a round of applause. An emcee said the next band would start in fifteen minutes.

Amy searched the crowd for Wren but couldn't find her. She headed to the concessions stand for water.

Amy was leaning against the stand, cooling off and scanning the crowd, when she saw a familiar face cross the stage. Wren! As the guitarist and bass player were plugging into amps, she grabbed the mic and pulled it down to her.

"Are you ready for The Verts?" Wren screamed.

The crowd roared in response.

Once the applause died down a hair below deafening, Wren yelled again, "This one's called 'Anaconda.'"

The music began, washing over the crowd like a tidal wave. The bass was so heavy, Amy could feel it pounding in her chest. Then Wren started to sing . . .

"Do you want me
Like I want you?
Do you need me
Like I need you?

Don't think this is a crush, the way I love. I'm an Anaconda, gonna eat you up.

Don't turn your back on the way I love. I'm an Anaconda, gonna eat you up."

Amy was amazed. Wren appeared to be a totally different person on stage. Her voice was amplified. Not just by the mic, but by confidence, similar to how Amy felt when she had her board under foot.

When Amy was strapped into her bindings, the snow slushing under her board, she felt like she could do anything in the world. That must be how Wren felt at this moment — at least that's how she acted up there.

"Do you want me
Like I want you?
Do you need me
Like I need you?

Don't think this is a crush, the way I love. I'm an Anaconda, gonna eat you up.
Don't turn your back on the way I love. I'm an Anaconda, gonna eat you up."

Amy was about to head back onto the dance floor when Dylan stepped out from the crowd. "We've got company," he said, leaning close to her, and then turning to the far side of the hall.

She followed his eyes to where four Collective agents stood. She gulped in fear, recognizing the tallest of them — the Corporal. After she had found her Fragment, he'd chased her down Four Directions Mountain. Only by sheer luck had she escaped.

"What's he doing here?" Amy whispered.

"I don't know," Dylan replied. "I thought I left Buzzer back on the streets of New York."

"Buzzer?" Amy said. "I'm talking about Corporal, the tall guy."

Dylan looked worried, and that frightened Amy because Dylan never worried about anything.

"This is bad," he said. "They're ganging up."

Amy reached into her pocket and pulled out the two-way radio.

"What are you doing?" Dylan asked.

"Calling for backup."

*　　*　　*

Back on shore, Eldrick and Gavin, the driver of the second watercraft, deposited the boys in the back seat of a rusted out Trans Am.

"You sure like to travel in style," Joey joked.

But peeking over Gavin's shoulder, Omar could see that you couldn't judge this car by its rust. Across the dash, there was a row of dials and buttons that Omar couldn't begin to guess the uses for. In front of Gavin, the glove box opened up into a small laptop computer. Its screen showed a map of the Twin Cities, and there was a red, flashing light toward the left half of the monitor.

"We've picked up a signal from Crow and Kestrel," Gavin said. "They're in downtown Minneapolis."

Crow and Kestrel? Omar wondered. *Those are the code names for Dylan and Amy.*

The car's engine roared to life.

"Buckle up, boys," said Eldrick.

Omar and Joey did as they were asked. Then they were off, just a blur speeding through the night.

8

After Amy hit the homing signal on their two-way, Dylan began pushing his way through the crowd. These quarters were just too tight for him, especially if trouble was brewing. He'd rather be somewhere where he could put four wheels on the pavement. That's when he was at his best, whether he had to flee or fight.

Amy held onto his shoulders as he wove through the crowd. He was beginning to like her, how brave she was. While Dylan would never dare let anyone know he was feeling afraid or worried, Amy's emotions were right on her sleeve. While Dylan couldn't help keep his emotions under wraps, she didn't care less what other folks thought.

It all goes back to living in foster homes and not knowing whom you could trust. Dylan never felt like he could let his guard down with anyone, yet around Amy, he felt his wariness of people, her specifically, growing into trust.

The doors were within sight when two figures loomed in front of Dylan — Buzzer and one of the female Collective agents.

"Dang!" Dylan cursed.

"Think I didn't recognize you under that ball cap?" Buzzer said with a laugh. "I let you get away earlier just so you could lead us to your little friend here." Buzzer nodded at Amy.

Looking back to see how Amy was doing, Joey saw Corporal and the other female Collective agent on either side of her. No escape.

"Uh-oh!" said Dylan.

"Now, you can do this the easy way, or you can do it my way," Buzzer said, grinding a fist into his meaty palm.

Dylan, without thinking, reached back with both hands to grab his board. A brilliant flash of blue electricity lit up the area as he brought his deck crashing down on the side of Buzzer's skull. Buzzer's knees buckled, and Dylan saw his chance to run.

"Come on, Amy," he shouted, failing to take the female Collective agent into consideration.

A flurry of small, rock-hard fists struck him in the face, the stomach, the chest, and the jaw. He reeled backwards in pain.

*   *   *

On stage, Wren felt alive. She didn't care that hundreds of people were watching her. Heck, she could barely see anyone with the blinding floodlights beating down on her from above. At the skatepark, attempting a trick, she may have floundered and been rewarded with a nasty raspberry while in front of a crowd of only a handful of people. Yet this is where she ruled. Here she was confident. Here she was queen. She knew she could sing. Sing loud and powerful. She could let all the fears and worries that caused her voice to constrict in her throat when she talked to people loosen up when she sang. For that reason, she thought it funny that they'd opened with the song "Anaconda."

As she sang, she scanned the crowd for Amy and her friend Dylan. Wren had purposely snuck off as they were dancing. She wanted to surprise her. She wanted to show Amy and her show-off friend that they weren't the only ones with some talent in this town.

"Do you want me
Like I want you?
Do you need me
Like I need you?

Don't think this is a crush, the way I love. I'm an
Anaconda, gonna eat you up.

Don't turn your back on the way I love. I'm an Anaconda,
gonna eat you up."

Wren spotted Amy and Dylan near the exit. They
were surrounded by four people dressed in black who
looked more serious, and more dangerous, than the
venue's bouncers. There was pushing and shoving,
and the crowd around them rippled. Dylan reeled back
under a torrent of blows from the smaller members
of the group. The tallest member of the foursome
confronted Amy. He held up a baton that emitted
crackling white energy at one end. He was about to
swing it down at her.

Wren screamed, "NOOOOOOooooooo!!!!!"

That word tore itself from her throat, amplified
beyond what any natural vocal chords could do, and hit
the Corporal like a semi. He was sent crashing to the
floor. Amy grabbed his Taser stick and turned it on
Dylan's attacker, who fell beside him.

Between the fight and Wren's scream, chaos erupted. A wall of people headed for the doors like a tsunami, carrying Amy and Dylan away from the Collective agents.

Wren stood on stage, her band members looking on, stunned at the confusion before them. Wren saw the tallest of the Collective members turn toward her. There was a frightening look of recognition in his gaze. She decided it was best that she hide.

Eldrick parked the car in front of First Ave. People were scattered and milling about everywhere.

"The show must have been a dud, if everyone's hanging out outside," Joey said.

"Or something happened in there," Gavin suggested.

Joey and Omar gulped. Their teammates where hopefully somewhere in that crowd of people.

"Okay, you three, hit the crowd and fan out," Eldrick said. "I'll stay with the car."

Omar, Joey, and Gavin jumped out of the car and dove into the mass of people. The crowd jostled Joey back and forth. Then he saw a familiar ball cap rush by. He reached out to grab the body that it was attached to.

Dylan whirled about, eyes wide with fear. Then he saw Joey.

"Joey!" Dylan shouted. "Man, are we glad to see you."

Behind him, Dylan dragged Amy along. She also looked frightened.

"Your limo's this way," Joey nodded toward Eldrick's car.

Upon seeing the rusted-out Trans Am, Dylan smiled at Joey's joke. Dylan, Joey, and Amy dove into the back seat. Soon, Omar squeezed in beside them. When Gavin hopped into the front seat, they were off.

The four teens looked each other over, wondering what sort of trouble each of them had found. Omar was wearing some crazy tie-dye. Joey smelled like stale fish. Dylan's right eye was swelling shut. And Amy had her hoodie pulled tight over her face. They kept quiet as the car roared through the streets of downtown Minneapolis, all painfully aware of the adults in the front seat who had come to their rescue. This isn't what any of them wanted, to be babysat. This was their first mission as a team, and they'd all wanted to pull it off without any outside help. They wanted to prove themselves worthy of being part of the Revolution.

Finally, Dylan broke the ice. "Anybody hungry?"

"Yeah, Eldrick," Joey piped up. "Can we hit a drive-through for some sliders?"

Joey elbowed Dylan. "Get it, Slider. Let's get some sliders!"

Dylan just rolled his eyes.

Then the stories of their day came spilling out, each more exciting than the next, threatening to drown out the other. Finally, Amy mentioned Wren's band and raved about her sign and even hummed some of the song, "Anaconda."

"Urk," Omar choked.

Amy, Joey, and Dylan turned toward Omar. His eyes had rolled back in his head, and he was having convulsions.

"Here we go again," Joey said.

10

At the mention of Wren's name, Omar's conscious mind was whisked away. He was surrounded in darkness. His hearing was his only sense that guided him. A scream rang in his ear — a girl screaming the note of a forgotten song.

Omar reached out a hand and felt a rocky cave wall. The wall seemed to pulse and move with the scream, as if the girl's singing was all that kept the rock from caving in around Omar and crushing him to death.

Eldrick's wrinkled mug was the first thing Omar saw when he came to.

"Welcome back to the real world," Eldrick said.

Omar sat up. He was still in the backseat of the rusted-out Trans Am.

Eldrick had pulled the car over into the parking lot of a fast food restaurant. His friends were standing outside the car, looking in at him. Concern was etched across their faces.

"It's her," Omar said. "Wren's the girl from my vision."

"How do you know?" Dylan asked.

"Did you see her skate?" Joey asked Amy.

"No, she's just a skatepark groupie," Amy replied.

"Listen," Eldrick cut in. "You've all had a rough day. Let's call it a night. Get some rest. Tomorrow we'll find her."

While what Eldrick had to say made sense, each of the four teens resented the fatherliness of his advice. This was still their mission. They would find Wren.

But only Omar was brave enough to speak up. "This is still our mission," he said, glancing at his companions and then back to Eldrick. "We'll find her."

Whether he was angered or proud at Omar's statement, Eldrick didn't react. He kept his cool and simply asked, "Okay, so who's hungry?"

*   *   *

The next day, none of them had completely overcome the fear of running into the Collective agents.

The group decided to stick together. *Safety in numbers*, Dylan thought. They were back at Brackett Skatepark. Omar was boarding, doing some casual tricks, grinds and ollies, nothing fancy, so as to fit in and not draw attention to himself. Joey and Amy sat on a bench just outside the skatepark's fence with BMX bikes lying at their feet.

Dylan was trying to mingle. He thought he recognized a few faces from yesterday, but every time he tried to start up a conversation, he got the brush off. Finally, he blocked a kid in the corner of the skatepark.

"Hey," Dylan said.

"Can I get past?" the kid said.

"I was just wondering if you'd know where I could find Wren?" Dylan asked. "I was here yesterday, talking to her, and . . ."

"Listen, just because you try to fit in, doesn't mean anyone here's going to talk to you," the kid replied. "We already dissed your friends."

"Friends? What?" Dylan was confused.

"You know, the men in black. They couldn't bully us into telling them Wren's whereabouts, and this new ploy's not gonna work either."

Dylan was about to protest when the kid shouldered his way past him.

He turned to pursue him, but as he did, Dylan was confronted by a wall of angry looking skaters.

"Get out of here," one of them shouted at Dylan.

All of a sudden, Omar was shoved through the crowd and stumbled next to Dylan, followed by Joey and Amy. The four of them stood in front of the angry mob of kids.

"And that goes for your friends, too!"

"We can take them," Dylan growled. Joey took the cue and stepped beside Dylan. Energy crackled in the air. If any one of them had noticed it, they would have seen it was a purplish hue instead of the electric blue they were used to.

"Chill," Omar said, placing one hand on each of their shoulders. "They aren't the bad guys. They're just trying to protect their friend. Let's go and check out the other skateparks — see if we have any better luck elsewhere."

Reluctantly, Joey and Dylan agreed and backed down. But they had similar results no matter where they went. They were recognized as outsiders, and nobody would talk to them. Some skaters even threatened them.

11

"So much for Minnesota nice," Joey grumbled.

The team was recuperating at the coffee shop that Joey and Omar had hung out at yesterday.

"So now what?" Dylan asked between sips of an iced coffee.

"We could go back to First Ave to see if anyone there would tell us something," Amy suggested.

"That's all the way across the metro," Joey said. "And we're on bikes and skateboards."

"Well, Wren is only one piece of the puzzle," Omar said. "There's still the caves. We never did get to investigate them. Maybe we could find something there."

"Sounds better than sitting around here," Joey said.

The team packed up their things, threw their packs over their shoulders, and headed out. Joey and Amy were on bikes, while Dylan and Omar tailgated on skateboards. The pace was a little mellower today, as Amy couldn't match Joey on a BMX.

Not to mention, they were each lost in their own thoughts. Amy feared that the Collective may have gotten to Wren. Dylan didn't share this with anyone, since he was still getting used to working as a team, but he'd seen what Wren did last night when she screamed at Corporal. Joey still thought he smelled like dead fish even though he had stolen some of Amy's herbal shampoo. And Omar wondered how the Collective knew so much about their plans when he had only shared his visions with his three companions and Eldrick.

Skyscrapers faded behind them as they crossed the Mississippi bridge. When they were just past the bridge's apex, Omar noticed the place where the sets of stairs led down to the island below. He had a thought.

"Hey, wait up," he called to his friends. "Let's head down to the island. I left a board down there last night."

Amy and Joey shouldered their bikes as Dylan and Omar led the way down the steps.

At the bottom step, Joey approached Omar. "You sure you're going back for a board?" Joey said.

"Whatcha mean?" Omar said.

"Hey, I saw that girl you were with yesterday, Omar," Joey said. "You were all James Bond-like with her."

Omar flushed. He had to admit, Shawna was more of a reason to head down to the island than a three-wheeled board. At least she was the one local that any of them had an in with — if she wasn't mad at him for ditching her in a canoe in the middle of the Mississippi River last night.

Omar ran over to the footbridge, and for good measure, pulled the abandoned board out from its hiding spot. Amy and Dylan didn't seem to notice anything fishy about this, but Joey was grinning from ear to ear.

"So you got what you came for," he said. "Can we go now?"

"There's one more thing," Omar said.

With feigned exasperation, Joey asked, "And whatever could that be?"

"There's this girl I met last night. She has friends who work at the T-shirt shop."

"What, where you bought that lovely tie-dye?" Joey asked.

"Enough," Omar growled.

Amy and Dylan watched the pair and shared a look of confusion as they followed Omar and Joey over to a T-shirt stand.

"Hey, Omar," Shawna shouted, popping up from behind the vendor tent. "I thought you ditched me for good last night." She ran up to Omar and gave him a friendly hug. Then she eyed up his friends.

"By the serious look of your friends, you aren't coming back to dance some more," Shawna said.

"Nah, I was hoping you could help us," Omar admitted.

"More cloak and dagger stuff?" Shawna asked. "Last night was fun until I got accosted by some of your other friends, if you know what I mean."

"They didn't hurt you, did they?" Omar asked.

"No, they just wondered why I was sneaking onto the island in a canoe," she explained. "Luckily, I have enough friends around here that they didn't bother pushing things."

"So what can I do you for?" she asked.

Omar quickly explained the situation. They were looking for a friend of theirs, Wren, who had also had a run-in with the Collective. She hadn't been seen since last night, and no one was willing to share her whereabouts.

"Well, some band members for this afternoon's show are backstage. Maybe they know her," Shawna said.

The five of them walked over to the stage, and then around back. Several people were sitting in lounge chairs — some eating snacks, others plucking mindlessly at instruments, and one or two just napping.

"Hey, look, it's Shawna," one of them said. "The tie-dye girl. Come to dress us for the show?"

Several chuckles greeted Shawna.

"Funny, Kurt. But today, I'm just wondering if you could help out my friends," Shawna said.

"We're looking for someone," Omar added. "Her name's Wren. She plays in a band called The Verts. Ever heard of them?"

"Hey!" One of the guys pointed at Amy. "You're that girl she was with." The guy stood up and walked over to them. He was short and muscular, and had that crazed bulldog look of a drummer.

"What?" Amy said, stunned.

"Yeah, you're her," the drummer continued.

"Do you know where she is?" Omar asked.

"She ditched us as soon as things turned crazy last night," the drummer said. "I haven't seen her since. She's probably holed up in the caves."

"The what?" Omar asked.

"The caves. That's where she lives," the drummer explained.

"Are you serious?" Amy asked.

"Yeah, she's been staying there ever since her folks kicked her out," the drummer said. "There's all sorts of hidden entrances around here. But I don't know which one she's in."

Omar thanked him for the information, and they all walked away with Shawna.

"Was he talking about the Wabasha Street Caves?" Joey asked Shawna.

"No, no, that place is basically a kitschy wedding hall. There are other entrances, secrets ones, where kids sneak in to party."

"How do we find these caves?" Amy asked.

Turning from Omar, Shawna answered. "I can show you."

12

Geared up with headlamps, gloves, and hiking boots,
Omar led the way as they climbed up a small ridge.
Shawna was by his side, helping him navigate. They
had already tried several caves with no luck. All they
found was discarded clothes, some ratty mattresses,
crushed cans, and the remains of several bonfires. Amy
couldn't imagine anyone staying — even for a night —
in any of those caves, let alone living in one. They were
disgusting, and Shawna had assured them that the caves
they had entered were some of the cleaner ones.

Shawna stopped and scanned the area. "I know
there's another entrance hidden around here
somewhere," she said.

The ridge was covered in trees and thick underbrush. The path they were on wasn't a path at all but a narrow dirt gully eroded away by water.

A sharp bird call drew Amy's attention skyward. There, she noticed a kestrel swooping through the trees. Then it landed on a pile of brush. For some reason, Amy knew it was a sign that this rare bird, her namesake bird, was here at this very moment.

"There," Amy said, pointing to the brush the kestrel had alighted on.

"Yeah, that's it," Shawna shouted. As she did, the bird flew away.

Omar and Shawna walked over to the brush pile. They pulled it away to reveal the mouth of a cave. Omar flicked on his headlamp and then stepped into the cave. Its ceiling was just high enough that he didn't have to crouch much. Shawna followed him, then Amy, and Joey and Dylan brought up the rear.

As they walked through the cave, the pair of boys behind her thought it was funny to make ghost noises and then grab Amy's shoulder or make headless shadows on the cave walls.

"One more time," Amy swore as Dylan whispered 'boo' in her ear, "And I'll rip both your heads off."

She was mad.

Amy was also worried about Wren, and feeling a little jealous of the connection that Omar and Shawna seemed to be sharing. She didn't like this, being the fifth wheel as Omar and Shawna pawed at each other every time one of them stumbled, and then Joey and Dylan buddied up behind her. She wished Wren were here. At least then she wouldn't feel like she didn't belong.

"Shhhh," Omar hushed Joey and Dylan. "There's someone up ahead."

They could hear quiet crying. Slowly, they wound their way past discarded furniture and trash. They rounded a bend and could see that the cave opened up into a small room.

"Wren!" Amy shouted.

Amy rushed past Shawna and Omar, knocking Omar aside. In the middle of the room Wren sat on a ratty bed. Her face was buried in her palms, and she was sobbing. Amy sat down next to her and wrapped her arms around Wren.

"It's okay," Amy whispered in Wren's ear.

Wren collapsed in her arms.

"Why are you staying here?" Amy asked.

Wren looked up, tears streaming down her face. "Just mad at my folks after we had a fight."

"But here?" Amy asked.

The filth of the cave surprised Amy. Broken glass, cigarette butts, and fast food wrappers littered the floor. In one corner were some moldy clothes. In another, the remains of a fire and some pots.

"They just don't understand me," Wren said, and broke down crying.

"Let's get you out of here," Amy said, about to stand, but Wren pulled her back down to the mattress.

"You shouldn't have come," Wren muttered.

Amy said, "We had to make sure you were okay."

Wren looked up into Amy's face. Her eyes were red and tears streaked her face.

"But it's not safe for you," Wren replied.

"What —?" before Amy could get out the question, she understood why. Out of the shadows stepped a dark figure — Corporal.

13

Corporal smiled down at Amy. "Glad we could witness this touching moment," he said.

Then Amy looked around the cave. Three more Collective agents had snuck out of the darkness. Wielding Taser sticks, they herded Joey, Dylan, and Shawna into the room.

Where's Omar, she wondered.

Sensing what everyone must have been thinking, Dylan joked, "So that's why you guys wear black. To lurk in the shadows like the creeps you are."

"Shut up," Buzzer yelled, and quicker than anyone could react, he slugged Dylan across the jaw, knocking him to the ground.

"That's for last night," Buzzer growled.

"That hurt," Dylan muttered, spitting blood from his cut lip.

Joey stood between Buzzer and Dylan to protect his friend.

"You're next," Buzzer spat.

What happened next took everyone by surprise. One of the Collective agents seemed to reach forward with his Taser stick and strike Buzzer. He dropped his Taser stick as the jolt knocked him to the ground, where he squirmed and thrashed.

"I-I-" the Collective agent stammered. "Somebody bumped me." And instinctively, that agent dropped his Taser stick. Once it hit the ground, Omar rose up from behind him and shoved him into the fourth Collective agent.

Corporal turned on them, but now Joey and Dylan both held Taser sticks.

"Looks like we're at an impasse here," Corporal laughed. "And I was wondering where you were."

Omar smiled at Amy. "When you rushed past me, you knocked me aside, and I stumbled and fell behind a rock. Everyone was so interested in seeing if Wren was okay, that nobody, not even you," Omar turned to Corporal, "noticed what had happened to me."

Joey, Dylan, and Omar squared off against the four Collective agents, with Amy and Wren caught in the middle. Each group now held two Taser sticks, and each group had a member — Dylan or Buzzer — who was a little worse for wear.

Amy said to Corporal, "All we want is Wren. Let's us have her, and we'll go."

"Can't do that," Corporal said.

"And why's that?" Amy asked.

"Ask Omar," Corporal said. "He knows why."

Amy turned to Omar, who stood with Joey and Dylan on either side of him. They looked formidable in the darkened cave, the situation wrenching their faces into a serious look.

"She's the key," Omar said. "She's the key to finding the next Fragment."

"Funny you should say key," said a Collective agent. "Because she is, in a literal sense."

Everyone looked at him, confused.

"You're talking crazy," Joey said.

"Just turn your light on the back wall there," the Collective agent said.

Omar did as he was told, while Joey and Dylan kept their Taser sticks at the ready. In the circle of light his headlamp created, there was an image of a hawk.

With the shadows of the rock wall, it almost looked as if it were alive and flying.

"That's why I've been living here," Wren said. "I can sense there's a power, somewhere, behind that image. It makes me feel safe."

"That power," the Collective agent added, "Is a Fragment. A Fragment that belongs to us."

"We'll see about that," Omar said.

"But how do we get it?" Amy asked.

"Wren," Omar said. "It's what my visions have been telling me. The power of her voice can open a portal through the rock."

Everyone now looked at Wren. The tears streaking down her face made her look helpless. But there was a spark of confidence behind her eyes. The same confidence that she displayed on stage as she sang.

"I'm not going to help them," Wren nodded toward the Collective agents. "I've already told them that."

"Well then, we have a problem," Corporal said. "Because no one's leaving this cave until you do. And should you get by us, the forest outside is thick with our agents."

Omar had a thought. Something he remembered from his past. Back home, when his friend Tommy was teaching him to skate, they would race down the pier.

There were always some stakes on who would get to the end of the pier first, whether it was fish tacos at the local stand or regreasing the others' wheel bearings. Bonus points for the best trick along the way.

"Let's race for it," Omar said.

"Huh?" Corporal cocked his head toward Omar.

"As you said, we're at a impasse. Wren won't sing for you, but she will for us. And you won't let her leave with us."

"So when she opens the portal, it'll be a free-for-all?"

"No, a race of champions — winner takes the Fragment — and then we all leave."

"Deal."

"You know, win or lose, they're not going to let us out of here alive," Amy whispered to Omar.

"One step at a time," Omar said. "Let's get the Fragment, and then figure that one out later."

"So who's your champion?" Joey asked.

"I am," Corporal replied. "And yours?"

Joey, Omar, Dylan, and Amy looked from one to another.

"I think you should do it," Dylan said to Omar.

"Yeah, you're kind of our leader," Joey said.

Omar looked at his companions, knowing that they had full faith in his abilities.

But something felt wrong about this, like it wasn't his race. Wasn't his battle. While Omar felt that it was his responsibility as leader of this group to take on the dangers that they faced, he knew he couldn't always protect his team members. On this mission, each of them had faced dangers and survived, and each of them had faced dangers prior to joining the Revolution. Each of them had also had past doubts that they'd had to overcome before finally gaining confidence in themselves and the group.

"Um, thanks for the vote of confidence," Omar said. "But I think Amy has some unfinished business here.

"What do you say, Ames?"

She gulped as if a giant bullfrog had just leaped down her throat.

"I-I-," she stumbled, then looking over at Wren, who looked so brave despite all that was going on, Amy regained her composure. "I got it."

"How fitting," Corporal said. "This'll be just like old times. But no one's going to save you this go-round."

Then Corporal smiled wickedly at her. "But now you'll need a board."

He pulled out a small sliver of wood from a zipper pocket on his jacket. It crackled with red energy as he held it.

"You have a Fragment," Joey gasped.

Corporal smiled. "Yeah, pried from the hands of one dead David Case."

Corporal looked over at Dylan. "Ring a bell?"

Detective Case had investigated the disappearance of Dylan's brother, Mikey, who had also been in possession of a Fragment — the one Dylan now had. Detective Case had also helped him out of a tight spot or two back in NYC as he was trying to recover the Fragment Mikey had.

The seriousness of their situation was starting to grow on all of them as they realized the Collective's reach was beyond their imagination, if it could get to anybody from their past.

"Now watch this," Corporal said.

He held the Fragment in front of him. It began to crackle more loudly and more brightly. Then in a flash, the Fragment went from being just a sliver of deck to a full-sized snowboard.

Everyone looked on in amazement.

Corporal turned to Amy. "Can you do that?"

KESTREL
VERSUS
CORPORAL

14

Omar watched the remaining Collective agents freak and scream at what had just happened. Buzzer was the first to the wall. He yanked on Corporal's hand. There was no give. Nothing. Corporal was planted in the rock solidly, as if the cave wall had formed around him.

"Corporal!" one of the other Collective agents cried.

That could have been Amy, Omar thought. *That could have been any one of us.*

The Collective agents were now chipping away and digging at the rock with whatever they could find — flashlights, jack knives, raw and bloodied fingers. Short of having a jack hammer in one of their back pockets, the effort was futile. Corporal was dead and buried.

What if one of my teammates died while I was in charge? Omar wondered, and the thought worried him. He'd never imagined that death would be part of joining the Revolution and pursuing its mission.

Joey was the voice of reason, pulling Omar from his musing. "Hey, Omar," he shouted. "Let's get while the getting's good."

Joey's comforting slap on the back was more of a push to get Omar moving in the right direction, toward the exit. Dylan and Wren were already disappearing around a turn in the cave.

"We need to find Amy," Omar said, regaining some of his composure.

"Yeah, you think that hawk was her?" Joey asked. "It felt like it was her."

"It had to be," Omar said. "I just don't want to imagine if it wasn't."

Omar dared one last glance back. The three collective agents were no longer digging. They had collapsed in front of the wall where Corporal's hand protruded and were sobbing softly. Omar felt that now was a good time to be out of there, before the Collective agents' despair turned to rage. An anger that would be directed at the people responsible for Corporal's death —Omar and his crew.

Dylan and Wren were the first to reach the cave's entrance. Omar and Joey were close behind. Shortly after leaving the portal room, Omar had signaled for Eldrick Otus to pick them up. Now that the mission had been achieved, he didn't mind calling in the cavalry. No use walking home when you could get a ride. Plus, he didn't want there to be any unpleasant surprises once they got out into the forest.

As they exited the cave, Eldrick was there waiting for them. While everyone else seemed happy to see him, Omar scowled at his mentor. Eldrick must have been tracking them. Otherwise, how would he have gotten here so quickly?

"Where's Amy?" Eldrick asked.

"There," Wren said, pointing to a tree branch high above them.

The hawk cocked its head toward them, looking at them first with one eye, and then the other. Deeming them safe, the hawk spread its wings and dove toward the ground.

Omar wasn't sure he believed what he saw, but as the hawk was only feet from the ground, its shape shifted, and warped, and grew. Wings became arms. Talons became feet. In the hawk's place, Amy landed on the ground, a little wobbly on her legs.

"Whoa," she said as she stumbled.

Dylan quickly put an arm around her to steady her.

"Wasn't sure how I was going to change back," Amy said. "But that worked."

"The hawk's power is in the air," Eldrick explained. "Once you land on the ground, you lose its power."

"Since when did you become so wise?" Joey asked.

The other teens laughed.

Gavin, who was in Eldrick's car at the bottom of the ridge, honked the horn, which drew everyone's attention back to the task at hand.

"The area's still thick with Collective agents," Omar said. "Let's find the quickest way out of here."

They all ran for the rusted-out Trans Am.

Once tucked in the back seat, next to Wren, Amy said, "We're going to take you home."

15

Joey, Dylan, and Amy were at their secret base, lounging on a sofa, watching some cartoons and taking a needed break from training.

Dylan leaned over to Amy. "Hey, can I see the decal again?"

Amy rolled up her left sleeve. It wasn't on her arm, where she had last seen it. So she rolled up her right sleeve. Still no decal. It was like a living tattoo. The decal was affixed to the surface of her skin, yet it wasn't attached to any one place. It drifted from calf to thigh to hip to back to shoulder to . . .

"Just take it off," Dylan said.

"No way," Amy shouted.

"Well, I want to see it," Dylan pleaded.

Amy opted to roll up one pant leg, and there it was, fluttering above her ankle. Dylan leaned in close to look at it. This was the very same hawk decal that had once adorned Tony Hawk's 900 board. Now it was stuck on Amy as if she were a wooden deck. Dylan reached out with one finger, slowly tracing its elaborate design.

Amy giggled. "That tickles."

Dylan jumped up.

"Whoa, cool!" he exclaimed.

On his wrist was the hawk decal, slowly flowing up his arm.

"Hey, give it back," Amy screeched.

"No way," Dylan said.

Joey reached over and clasped Dylan's arm, just above where the decal was. As it moved up Dylan's arm, to where Joey's hand was, the decal transferred from Dylan to Joey.

"Hey," Dylan exclaimed. "Give it back."

Dylan leaped on Joey, trying to touch the hawk decal before it slid under Joey's shirt. They began to wrestle, and Amy quickly joined the fray. Arms flailed and feet kicked as they rolled about on the floor.

They only stopped when Eldrick burst through the door. Omar was right behind him.

They stood amazed as they watched the hawk decal slide from Joey's back to the knee Amy had used to pin him down.

"I was wondering why you were able to be in possession of two Fragments," Eldrick said to Amy. "Apparently, this one has chosen you as a group."

Omar leaned down to the decal on Amy's leg. He reached out to touch it. The hawk transferred to his hand. As soon as it did, Omar bolted up straight. His eyes rolled in the back of his head, and he began to quiver.

"Here we go again," Joey said. "Omar's in vision mode."

Theresa Davis_
CODE NAME: WREN

AGE: 16

HOMETOWN: Minneapolis, MN

SPORT: Skateboarding

INTERESTS: Singing, Rock Music

BIO: Wren's a newb on the skateboard but a pro on stage. A lot of the local skaters are fans of her band The Verts, so she hangs out at the skateparks with them. One of her favorites is Bracket Skate Park in Minneapolis. Her band mates have even taught her some basic tricks like grinds and kick flips. If she's not on her board, she can be found on stage at one of the Twin Cities' underage clubs, belting out tunes that she wrote for her band—they play all originals. Currently, she's homeless because of an argument with her folks.

STORY SETTING: Midwest

ABOUT TONY HAWK

TONY HAWK is the most famous and influential skateboarder of all time. In the 1980s and 1990s, he was instrumental in skateboarding's transformation from fringe pursuit to respected sport. After retiring from competitions in 2000, Tony continues to skate demos and tour all over the world.

He is the founder, President, and CEO of Tony Hawk Inc., which he continues to develop and grow. He is also the founder of the Tony Hawk Foundation, which works to create skateparks and empower youth in low income communities.

TONY HAWK WAS THE FIRST SKATEBOARDER TO LAND THE 900 TRICK, A 2.5 REVOLUTION (900 DEGREES) AERIAL SPIN, PERFORMED ON A SKATEBOARD RAMP.

ABOUT THE AUTHOR_

BLAKE A. HOENA grew up in central Wisconsin, where, in his youth, he wrote stories about robots conquering the Moon and trolls lumbering around in the woods behind his parents house. Later, he moved to Minnesota to pursue a Masters of Fine Arts degree in Creative Writing from Minnesota State University, Mankato. Since graduating, Blake has written more than forty books for children.

AUTHOR Q & A_

Q: DO YOU PARTICIPATE IN ACTION SPORTS? HOW HAVE THEY INFLUENCED YOU?

A: I like to hit trails with my mountain bike. After a hard, sweaty ride, I feel pretty relaxed and clear-headed. Then I can sit at my computer to crank out a few hundred words.

Q: DESCRIBE YOUR APPROACH TO THE TONY HAWK'S 900 REVOLUTION SERIES.

A: I haven't been on a skateboard since before Tony Hawk did his celebrated 900, so I started off by watching A LOT of YouTube videos of different tricks to get some ideas.

Q: ANY FUTURE PLANS FOR THE TONY HAWK'S 900 REVOLUTION SERIES?

A: Yeah, I'm writing Volume 9 in the series. I wanted to do a post-apocalyptic story, where Omar has a vision of what the world would be like if the Collective won. And yes, there will be zombies!

TONY HAWK'S
900 revolution

TONY HAWK'S 900 REVOLUTION, VOL. 5: AMPLIFIED

As a new chapter begins, the first four members of the Revolution team — Omar, Dylan, Amy, and Joey — search for next piece of Tony Hawk's powerful 900 skateboard. Their journey takes them to the American Midwest, where a rock-n-roll teen named Wren tunes in to the mysterious Fragment's location. Unfortunately, when another gang of teens, known as the Collective, follows them on their quest, the dangers are suddenly amplified.

TONY HAWK'S 900 REVOLUTION, VOL. 6: TUNNEL VISION

As the team finds more pieces of th 900 skateboard, the skills of eac member are suddenly magnifie For Omar Grebes, this surge power creates a flood of psych visions about the locations o the Fragments and the orig of their mysterious powers. He determined to find the rest of th missing pieces as fast as possibl Unfortunately, Omar's tunn vision quickly leads to whirlwind of trouble for the tear

QUEST CONTINUES...

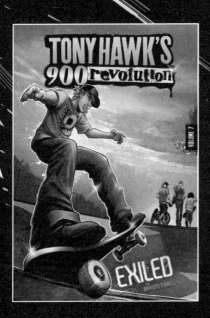

TONY HAWK'S 900 REVOLUTION, VOL. 7: EXILED

Every time the Revolution team finds another piece of the mysterious 900 skateboard, a gang of troublesome teens, known as the Collective, is close behind — and another encounter could be deadly! Omar, Dylan, Amy, and Joey suspect that one of them must be a double-crossing snitch. Soon, these suspicions begin to splinter the Revolution. Only one solution can save the team and their vital quest — send the main suspect into exile!

TONY HAWK'S 900 REVOLUTION, VOL. 8: LOCKDOWN

With Dylan Crow in exile and the others on lockdown, the Revolution team is falling apart fast — and their enemies are picking up the pieces! With each new Fragment, the gang of troublesome teens, known as the Collective, grows more powerful. And, when Elliot Addison, a new member of the Collective, steals the Revolution's cache of Fragments, all hope seems lost. If the team can't pull themselves together, the Revolution might be overthrown by evil.

TUNNEL VISION

Omar sat on a cold, metal table in the facility's infirmary. Eldrick Otus, the silver-haired leader of the Revolution, scrutinized the burn on Omar's hand.

"This was caused by the Fragment?" Eldrick asked.

"Yeah," Omar answered. "It was like being struck by lightning. I lost feeling in my arm for a while, too."

"I've never seen anything like this before. A Fragment striking a Key . . . it's unheard of."

"Well, my hand would beg to differ."

Eldrick scoured a nearby table until he found ointment, a cotton swab, a square bandage, and a roll of white tape. As he began to dress Omar's injury, he said, "Have your visions become more focused? More vivid?"

Omar had not told anyone of the startling, intense visions he'd had in Italy. "Um . . ." he started.

Eldrick already knew the answer.

"Yeah," Omar finally admitted. "Major league visions. They felt almost real."

Eldrick nodded. "That's what I was afraid of."

"Wait, so you knew this would happen?"

"No." Eldrick applied the bandage and began to wrap Omar's hand in the smooth, white tape. "It was an assumption that has unfortunately proven true."

"Sounds like semantics, old man," Omar said. "Give it to me straight."

"As you've seen —" Eldrick indicated the pulsating wheel attached to Omar's deck, which leaned against a nearby chair, "— each Fragment of the 900 board comes with an alarming amount of power. It's easy to manage, and simple to control. However, as our mission progresses, the bonds between your friends and the Fragments are strengthening. And so is their potential."

"The more pieces we find, the stronger we become?"

"Yes."

"And my visions will only get worse?"

"They'll become more specific, yet uncontrolled." Eldrick wrapped the final strip of white tape around Omar's wrist. "Now, do you remember what you saw?"

"How could I forget?" Omar told Eldrick of the blinding light, the mountain, and the snake. He wasn't sure why, but he decided to keep Tommy's identity as the serpent in his vision a secret.

Read more in the next adventure of . . .

Tony Hawk's 900 Revolution

TONY HAWK'S
900 revolution